Superhero HARRY

written by **RACHEL RUIZ**

illustrated by **STEVE MAY**

Capstone Young Readers
a capstone imprint

Superhero Harry is published by Capstone Young Readers
A Capstone Imprint
1710 Roe Crest Drive
North Mankato, Minnesota 56003
www.mycapstone.com

Copyright © 2018 by Capstone Young Readers

Library of Congress Cataloging-in-Publication Data is
available on the Library of Congress website.

ISBN: 978-1-62370-886-3

Designer: Hilary Wacholz

Printed and bound in China.
010713/S18

TABLE OF CONTENTS

ALL ABOUT
Superhero
HARRY

NAME: Harrison Albert Cruz

FAVORITE COLOR: red

FAVORITE FOOD: spaghetti

FAVORITE SCHOOL SUBJECT: science

HOBBIES: playing video games, inventing, and reading

IDOLS: Albert Einstein and Superman

BEST FRIEND, NEIGHBOR, AND SIDEKICK: Macy

The Superhero Project

CHAPTER 1

BIRTHDAY BOY

Today is super special. It is Harry's first day of school. It is also his birthday!

"Harry!" his mom calls. "Time to get up!"

But Harry has been up for an hour. He's working on X-ray vision goggles. They are his latest invention.

"Just a minute!" Harry yells.

Harry likes superheroes. He
also likes inventing things. So
Harry invents things to make
him more like a superhero.

The problem is, Harry's inventions usually don't work. The other problem is that Harry is clumsy. These are two big problems if you are trying to be a superhero.

Once Harry invented a cool supersonic flying machine. He used it to fly off his bed. And he fell flat on his face.

Another time Harry made superhero suction shoes. He used them to climb to the top shelf of the hall closet to look at hidden presents.

But the suction on the shoes
didn't stick. Down went Harry.

But these failures don't stop
Harry. He needs super inventions to
be a superhero. Superheroes don't
give up, and neither does Harry.

"Amazing Macy to Superhero Harry. Come in, Superhero Harry. Over."

"Copy that, Amazing Macy. Superhero Harry here. Over," Harry replies.

Macy lives in the apartment building next door. In addition to being Harry's neighbor, she's his superhero sidekick, classmate, and best friend.

"Superhero Harry, you have an incoming. I repeat, you have an incoming. Over," Macy says into her walkie-talkie.

Harry's happy to see that
Macy is using the pulley system
he invented last week.

When the bucket reaches Harry's window, he pulls out a card. It is covered with glitter glue and superhero stickers.

"Thanks, Macy!" Harry shouts.

"Use your walkie-talkie!" she yells back.

"Thanks, Macy! Over!" Harry says into his walkie-talkie.

"See you at the bus stop. It's going to be a super day! Over and out!" Macy says.

"It's the first day of school AND my birthday," Harry says. "How could today be anything but super?"

CHAPTER 2

THE FIRST DAY

At school Ms. Lane crowns Harry student of the day. The entire class sings to him. He even gets to pass out birthday treats at the end of the day. While everyone is eating, Ms. Lane makes an announcement.

"I have your first assignment," she says.

"Already?" Macy says.

"Yes, already. How are you a superhero in your everyday life?" Ms. Lane asks. "That is your assignment. Make a presentation to show the class on Friday."

That doesn't give me much time, Harry thinks.

"Everyone will vote on the best presentation. The winner will get a special prize," Ms. Lane says.

The final bell rings. Harry can't wait to get home. He'll get to open gifts and eat cake. Then he can start his superhero project!

* * *

"A real live inventor set!"

Harry says as he opens a gift. "It

says I can invent my own robot!

Thanks Mom and Dad!"

"It's my turn!" Aunt Gwen says.

Harry opens her gift and starts screaming with excitement.

Aunt Gwen's gift is the most beautiful thing Harry has ever seen. It's a shiny red superhero cape. It has a gold lightning bolt on the back.

"Harry, this cape will give you superpowers," Aunt Gwen says. "You just have to believe in yourself."

"For real live life?" Harry asks.

"For real live life," Aunt Gwen says, smiling.

"I'm going to use the cape to help me win the superhero assignment contest at school," Harry says.

"What are you going to do?" his dad asks.

"Oh nothing much," Harry says. "Just invent my greatest superhero invention ever!"

CHAPTER 3

THE ANNOYING DAY

The next morning Harry is really tired. He stayed up too late working on his project.

"Harry! Wake up! You're going to be late for school!" Mom yells.

Oh, no! Harry overslept! He jumps out of bed and puts on his favorite shirt. As he puts his arm through the sleeve, it rips. Harry quickly finds another shirt.

"Harry! The bus is here!" his mom calls.

Harry zooms to the kitchen. As he runs out the door, his mom hands him a muffin.

Harry tries to stuff his superhero cape into his backpack as he rushes toward the bus. But the zipper breaks. His cape tumbles out. It lands in a mud puddle.

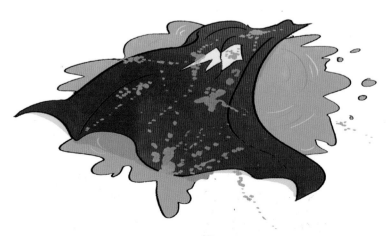

"Oh, no!" Harry says. He picks up the cape and tries to clean it off. It doesn't work. And now he has mud all over his shirt too.

Once on the bus Macy waves Harry over. Harry dumps his stuff on the seat.

"What happened to your shirt?" Macy asks.

"Don't ask," Harry says as he sits down, right on his muffin.

Things do not get better at school. Harry trips in the hall. He drops his lunch tray. He forgets his math homework. Harry is so glad when the final bell rings.

* * *

At dinner Harry tells his parents about his tough day.

"Sounds like quite a day," his mom says.

"It really was. But it's time to put that behind me. I need to focus on my superhero invention. It's going to be the best! I know I'm going to win," Harry says.

"I'm glad you're taking your
assignment so seriously," his
mom says. "But I think you may
be missing the point."

"The point?" Harry asks.

"Your teacher asked how you're a superhero in your *everyday* life," Harry's dad says. "I think she's looking for something regular people can do."

"It doesn't have to be an invention," his mom adds.

"Sorry, Mom and Dad," Harry says. "Ms. Lane asked about superheroes, and superheroes use superpowers. It's just that simple."

CHAPTER 4

THE ASSIGNMENT

"Who would like to give the first presentation?" Ms. Lane asks.

Macy and Melanie jump right up. Melanie takes her shoes off.

"Macy and I are on the same gymnastics team," Melanie says. "For weeks I've been trying to do a back handspring. I just couldn't get it. Macy helped me practice every day until — "

"She learned how to do it!"
Macy yells.

Melanie does her back
handspring. Macy stays close
in case she needs help.

"Wonderful, girls!" says Ms. Lane. "You're both superheroes. Macy helped a friend with her goal. And Melanie worked hard and didn't give up."

Violet reads a story about helping her grandmother clean her house.

Ethan sings a song about cleaning up the park with his scout group.

They all did the assignment wrong, Harry thinks. *You can't be a superhero if you don't use superpowers!*

Finally it is Harry's turn.

He carries a box to the front of the room. He pulls out a pair of shiny silver puffy boots. They each have lightning bolts and a battery pack.

"These are my superhero rocket blaster boots. They will blast me to the moon. Or at least really, really high," Harry says.

"Cool!"

"Let's see Harry!"

"Turn them on!"

"Blast to the moon!"

Harry beams. He puts on his cape. He slips into the boots and turns on the battery packs. He stands tall. And he waits.

And waits some more.

Nothing happens.

"Let me try that again," Harry says. He turns the battery packs off and on.

But still, nothing happens. He looks at his classmates. Everyone is staring at him.

"I don't understand," Harry says. "I really thought they would work."

Harry knows he will never win the contest now.

CHAPTER 5

THE RESULTS

Ms. Lane counts all the votes. The winner for the best superhero assignment presentation is Elle.

Elle showed she's a superhero by organizing a sock drive. She got people to donate socks for people in need. She collected more than 100 pairs!

Ms. Lane calls Harry up to her desk.

"Do you understand why you didn't win?" she asks.

"Because my rocket blaster boots didn't work," Harry says. "But they are really cool."

"Harry, your boots are very cool," Ms. Lane says. "But they didn't show me how you *really* are a superhero."

"But Ms. Lane," Harry says, "they are my *superhero* rocket blaster boots. They have the word *superhero* in the actual name!"

"Harry, being a superhero isn't just about inventions. It is about helping others," Ms. Lane says.

Harry thinks about all of the presentations. Each one was about someone helping someone else. Maybe his parents were right after all.

"So you don't have to have superpowers to be a superhero?" he asks.

"Nope. You can be a hero in a lot of ordinary ways," Ms. Lane says. "Do you understand?"

"That makes sense," Harry says. "But I'm still going to make inventions and try to fly and all that kind of stuff."

"And that's what makes you so super, Harry," his teacher says. "You never give up."

"Of course not!" Harry says. "See you tomorrow, Ms. Lane. Superhero Harry, over and out!"

The Recess Bully

CHAPTER 1

HARRY'S SUPER HALLOWEEN COSTUME

Harry can't wait to get to school today! It's Halloween! There's going to be a party and a costume parade around school.

Harry's dressing up as Superman. His costume is almost complete. He's wearing his favorite red superhero cape from his aunt Gwen. Now he's just adding the finishing touch.

Harry loves superheroes. He wishes he had superpowers. If he had superpowers, he probably wouldn't be so clumsy.

But since he doesn't, he builds inventions to make himself more superhero-ish.

His latest invention is his superhero flashlight belt. He made it using one of his old belts, small flashlights, and rubber bands. When he presses a button, the flashlights turn on. It helps Harry find things.

"There it is!" Harry yells, reaching for his superhero mask under his bed.

When Harry gets on the school bus, a girl dressed like Wonder Woman waves him over.

"Harry, over here!"

That's Macy. She is Harry's next-door neighbor, superhero sidekick, classmate, and best friend.

As Harry walks toward Macy, he trips on his cape. His apple rolls right out of his lunch bag and under a seat.

"Your apple!" Macy says.

"Not to worry," Harry says. "I'll find it with this."

Harry presses the button, and his superhero flashlight belt lights up. He finds the apple in a flash.

"Wow!" Macy says. "You really are like a superhero."

CHAPTER 2

THE NEW KID AT SCHOOL

At Parker Elementary everyone's wearing Halloween costumes. Melanie is a mermaid. Jackson is a cowboy.

Even Ms. Lane is wearing a costume. She is dressed like Dorothy from *The Wizard of Oz*. She's wearing ruby slippers and carrying a basket with a plush dog inside.

"Class," Ms. Lane says, "we have a new student joining us today. Please say hello to Jeremy."

"Hi, Jeremy!" the class says.

Jeremy is not wearing a costume. And he doesn't look very happy.

"Hey, Jeremy, where's your costume?" Harry asks. "Are you going to put it on after lunch?"

"What are going to be?" Macy asks.

Jeremy's response surprises Harry and Macy.

"Costumes are lame. Halloween is lame. And this school is super lame," he says, sliding down in his seat.

"Today is your first day at Parker Elementary," Macy says. "How do you know you won't like it here?"

"Just a feeling I get," Jeremy says. He looks at Harry. "What are you supposed to be anyway?"

"I'm Superman, of course!" Harry says proudly, pretending to flex his super muscles.

"His nickname is Superhero Harry," Macy explains. "And Superman is his favorite superhero."

"Superhero Harry? More like Superlame Harry!" Jeremy says as he laughs.

"Hey, that's mean," Macy says, but Jeremy turns his back to her.

Harry and Macy look at each other. Harry just shrugs.

CHAPTER 3

THE RECESS BULLY

At recess things with Jeremy don't get any better. Harry and some of his classmates are playing kickball. But not Jeremy. He's sitting under a tree alone.

"Hey, Jeremy! Why don't you join us?" Macy asks.

"Sure," Jeremy says.

"Great!" Macy says. "You can be on my team."

But instead of playing, Jeremy runs over and steals the ball. "Try playing kickball now!" he yells.

"Hey!" Ethan cries. "Bring that back!"

"What is up with that kid?" Macy asks.

"I don't know," Harry says. "But as our class superhero, I will save the day. I promise."

Harry finds Jeremy on the other side of the playground.

"That wasn't very nice, Jeremy. Can you please give me the ball back?" Harry asks.

"You'll have to find it first,"
Jeremy says.

Harry does a quick scan of the
playground. He doesn't see the ball
anywhere.

"Why don't you just use your X-ray vision to find the ball, Superman?" Jeremy asks.

That's when Harry remembers he's wearing his superhero flashlight belt! Harry presses the button, and the belt lights up.

"What is that ridiculous thing?" Jeremy asks.

"It's my superhero flashlight belt," Harry replies. "It's going to help me find the ball you took."

"Superhero flashlight belt?" Jeremy laughs. "You are super weird!"

This makes Harry even more determined to find the ball. He shines his belt toward the bushes. He immediately spots the ball.

"Found it!" Harry calls to Macy and the other kids.

"Whatever," Jeremy says as he walks away.

Harry happily brings the ball back to his friends.

CHAPTER 4

SUPERHERO HARRY WILL SAVE THE DAY

The next day at recess, things get even worse. First Jeremy steals Violet's jump rope and buries it. Then he takes Ethan's hat and hides it in a pile of leaves.

When Harry tries to get back his friends' things, Jeremy teases him. He calls him a nerd because he likes superheroes, science, and inventing stuff.

"We should tell Ms. Lane Jeremy is being a bully," Macy says.

"Not yet. Superhero Harry can still save the day," Harry says. "I just need to keep thinking."

* * *

At dinner, Harry is not hungry.

"I forgot the salad dressing," Harry's mom says.

"I'll get it!" Harry says. He runs to the kitchen and then runs back at top speed.

His mom says, "Please don't run or you'll drop the —"

SPLAT!

Harry cleans up the mess and
sits back down.

"What's wrong?" his dad asks.

Harry tells his parents about
the mean things Jeremy has been
doing and saying.

"Superhero is part of my
nickname, but I can't even defend
myself or my friends against a
bully. What kind of superhero is
that?" he asks.

"Have you tried talking to
Jeremy?" his mom asks.

"Kind of," Harry says. "He just ignored me. Then he was mean again."

"I think you should try again," his dad says.

"If that doesn't work, you need to tell your teacher what's going on," his mom says.

But Harry thinks his parents are wrong. He's sure only one of his superhero inventions can stop Jeremy from being a bully. He has a long night of inventing ahead of him.

CHAPTER 5

RECESS? NO THANKS.

The next day when the bell rings for recess, nobody moves.

"Time for recess," Ms. Lane says.

"No thanks, Ms. Lane," Violet says. "I think I'll stay inside and paint a picture."

"I'm going to build a fort," Ethan says. "An inside fort."

"Me too," says Melanie.

"Me three," Jackson says.

Harry and Macy know why their friends don't want to go outside for recess.

"So nobody wants to go out for recess?" Ms. Lane asks, surprised.

They hear a loud thunderclap outside, and then rain starts to pour.

"Well then," Ms. Lane says. "I guess everyone will have indoor recess today."

"Hooray!" everyone shouts.

Ms. Lane says she has to step out for a few minutes. When she's gone, Harry gathers everyone around. Everyone except Jeremy, that is.

"We need to do something," Harry says. "We can't let Jeremy ruin recess for us."

"But what can we do?" Violet whispers.

"Yeah, you keep saying you'll save the day," Melanie says. "What's your plan?"

"It's this," Harry says, pulling something from his backpack.

"What is that?" Jackson asks.

"It's my latest superhero invention. I made it using my old bike pump and some confetti," Harry explains.

"Does it work?" Macy asks. "I mean, have you actually tried it on someone?"

"No, but I know it will work. The next time Jeremy does something mean, I'll pump confetti at him. Confetti always puts people in a good mood," Harry says.

"You can't be a bully if you're in a good mood," Macy says.

"Harry, you might actually save the day," Ethan says.

"I sure hope so," Harry says. "After all, I *am* Superhero Harry!"

"What are you guys whispering about?" Jeremy asks.

"Nothing," Macy says.

Jeremy pulls Macy's Wonder
Woman tiara-headband off her
head. He throws it across the room.

"Why don't you just go away and leave us alone!" Violet yells. "Nobody likes you!"

Harry is about to use his new invention and pump confetti all over Jeremy. But he stops.

Jeremy is crying.

CHAPTER 6

FROM BULLY TO FRIEND

"What is going on in here?" Ms. Lane asks, walking back into the classroom.

"Everyone is bullying me," Jeremy says.

"That's not true!" Macy yells.

"He's lying!" Harry shouts.

"Calm down, class," Ms. Lane says. "Jeremy, are your classmates *really* bullying you?"

Everyone looks at Jeremy. His face starts turning red. He looks down at his feet.

"No," Jeremy quietly says.

"I've been bullying them."

"It's never okay to be a bully," Ms. Lane says.

"I know. It's just something I do," Jeremy says.

"I yelled at him and made him cry, Ms. Lane," Violet says. "I'm really sorry, Jeremy."

"It's fine," Jeremy says.

"Okay, class. Let's get back to recess," Ms. Lane says. "Jeremy, please come see me for a minute."

Harry remembers the advice his parents gave him at dinner. He stops Jeremy. Macy stays next to Harry.

"Jeremy, why have you been so mean to all of us?" Harry asks.

"My family moves around a lot," he explains. "It's a lot easier to leave if I don't have any friends. I learned that after my third school."

"It must be hard to always be the new kid," Macy says.

"We'd like to be friends with you, no matter how long you stay here," Harry says.

"Really?" Jeremy asks. "You want to be my friend even after I've been bullying you?"

"If you stop being a bully we would love to be your friends," Macy says.

"I'd like that," Jeremy says.

"So would I. Mission complete! Superhero Harry, over and out!"

The
Runaway
Robot

CHAPTER 1

CHORES! BLAH!

It's Saturday! Harry leaps out of bed. He has a full day planned.

After breakfast, he'll ride his bike to the park. This afternoon, his dad is taking him to see the new Superman movie. And after dinner, he'll work on his latest superhero invention.

Harry loves superheroes. He wishes he had real superpowers. But he doesn't, so he creates superhero inventions to make him more superhero-ish.

One time Harry made a super suctionator. It was supposed to pick up Harry's Legos. Instead, it picked up the cat.

Another time Harry made a super tooth brusher. It was supposed to brush Harry's teeth for him. Instead, it squirted toothpaste in his eyes and tried to brush his eyebrows!

It seems like Harry fails at all of his attempts to be super. But Harry never stops trying.

"Harry!" his mom calls. "Before you go out, you have to finish your chores."

Oh, right. Chores. Harry had purposely forgotten about those. Harry quickly cleans his room and the big fish tank.

Before he heads for the door, Harry puts on his favorite superhero boots with the lightning bolts. They're a little too big on him, but he wears them anyway.

"Be back soon, Mom!" he calls.

"Harry, can you please take

the garbage on your way out?"

Mom asks.

In his apartment building, the garbage chute is way at the end of the hall.

As Harry runs down the hall, he trips over his boots. He drops the garbage bag and spills garbage everywhere. Split pea soup from last night's dinner splats all over his shirt, pants, and his favorite boots.

Harry's had it with chores! He knows exactly what his next superhero invention is going to be, and it's going to be awesome.

CHAPTER 2

MEET SUPER ROBY

On Sunday Harry wakes up extra early to finish working on his latest invention.

It's a real live robot! Harry used his robot kit from his birthday to start it. Then he added a few of his own things to make the robot extra useful.

"Super Roby, you look awesome!" Harry says. "Now let's see if you work."

Harry dumps his hamper of dirty clothes onto his bedroom floor.

"Here goes nothing!" Harry pushes some buttons on a remote control. Then he waits.

Super Roby starts picking up the clothes!

"Awesome!" Harry yells. "Now let's see if you can put the clothes into the basket."

Harry pushes more buttons.

Once again, Super Roby does

as he's commanded.

"Woo-hoo!" Harry shouts.

"Super Roby really works!"

"Amazing Macy to Superhero Harry. Come in, Superhero Harry. Over."

Macy is Harry's neighbor. She's also his superhero sidekick, classmate, and best friend. She lives across the courtyard.

"Copy that, Amazing Macy. Superhero Harry here. Over."

"Bad news. I can't come over to work on our super secret hideout today. Over," replies Macy.

"Why not? Over," Harry says.

"I have to reorganize the playroom. It's a mess! Over."

Harry says, "I don't have to worry about doing chores anymore. Over."

"What do you mean? Over," replies Macy.

"I invented a robot to do my chores for me. Over."

"Does it actually work? Over," asks Macy.

"You'll see for yourself tomorrow," Harry says. "I'm bringing him to the class science fair. Over and out!"

* * *

After breakfast, Harry's mom asks, "Can you please sweep the kitchen floor?"

"No problem, Mom!" Harry says.

"Thank you, Harry," his mom says.

Harry puts the broom in Roby's hands. Then he pushes some buttons on the remote control. *Shazam!*

Super Roby is sweeping the kitchen floor! Harry kicks his feet up while he reads a superhero comic book.

"This is the life," Harry says.

CHAPTER 3

SUPER ROBY RULES

"Okay, class," Ms. Lane says. "It's time to present your science projects. When everyone is done we will vote, and I will announce the winner."

Violet goes first. She made a toy race car out of a plastic soda bottle. She used bottle caps for wheels and a computer battery to make it run.

Ethan is next. He added an elevator to his sister's dollhouse. He shows how it moves up and down with a remote control.

Then it's Macy's turn. She made magnetic superhero wrist cuffs. When she holds them up, Ms. Lane's paper clips move her way.

It's finally Harry's turn. He wheels Roby to the front of the room.

"This is Super Roby. That's short for Superhero Robot," Harry says proudly.

"What does Super Roby do?" Melanie asks.

"What would you like him to do?" Harry asks.

"Can he take this broken pencil to the trashcan?" Melanie asks.

Harry puts the broken pencil in Super Roby's hand. He pushes some buttons on his remote.

Super Roby goes to toss the pencil away. His robot actually works!

"Should Super Roby erase the white board?" Harry asks, picking up an eraser.

"Sure, Harry," Ms. Lane says. "Or should I say, Super Roby."

"Now this something I have to see!" Violet says.

Harry places the eraser in Super Roby's grip. He pushes some buttons on his remote control. Super Roby moves the eraser back and forth across the board.

"Harry, I am super impressed,"
Ms. Lane says. "Please tell us how
you made your robot. How does
he work?"

"It's simple, I just use this remote control —"

That's when Harry's remote control starts making weird noises. The buttons light up, but Harry is not pushing them.

"Hey! Super Roby took my water bottle!" Serena yells. "And he's heading out the door!"

CHAPTER 4

ROBOT ON THE LOOSE

"Sorry, Serena! That wasn't supposed to happen," Harry says. "I'll get your water bottle back. After all, I'm Superhero Harry, and I will save the day!"

Then he asks, "Ms. Lane, can I go chase my robot?"

"Please Harry, and hurry!" she says.

Once in the hallway, Harry doesn't see Super Roby anywhere. Then he hears someone yell.

"A robot just dumped a bottle of water in my lap!"

Harry runs in the direction of the voice. He reaches Mr. Kent's classroom.

"Any chance you've seen a robot lately?" Harry asks.

"We certainly did," Mr. Kent says. "He rolled in here and made a huge mess! His lights were blinking, and he was making loud noises."

"Do you know which direction that crazy robot went? I have to stop him," Harry says.

"That way!" all the kids yell.

Harry takes off again.

"Help! That robot took all of my chocolate chip cookies!" a kid yells.

Uh-oh! When Harry reaches Mr. Stark's classroom, Super Roby is there. He's smashing chocolate chip cookies against his head! He's making a big mess!

"Who is responsible for this runaway robot?" Mr. Stark asks.

"I am, sir, but I can't seem to stop him," Harry says. "The remote control just went crazy. Wait, where is the remote control?"

"Harry, there you are!" Macy says, running into Mr. Stark's classroom. "I have your remote!"

"Your robot is pulling papers out of our mailboxes," a boy says.

Papers are flying everywhere.

"What am I going to do, Macy? Harry asks.

"You made Super Roby, and you can fix him," Macy says.

"You're right," Harry says.

"Just think about how you built him," Macy says. "And then go backward."

"Your robot just left," Mr. Stark says. He looks really annoyed.

"Don't worry," Harry says. "I know how to stop him!"

CHAPTER 5

EVEN SUPERHEROES DO CHORES

Harry and Macy race back to their classroom. Super Roby is there too, and he's causing more chaos.

"Your robot just scribbled all over my test!" a girl yells.

"I'm really sorry. But I think I figured out how to stop him," Harry says. "Macy, hold him in place."

"He's a little out of control," Macy says. "I may need some help."

"Right," Harry says. "Macy, can you hold his hands? Ms. Lane, can you hold him in place?"

"I'm happy to help, Harry," Ms. Lane says.

Macy grabs the robot's hands. Ms. Lane grabs his body. Harry tinkers with some wires.

"I created Super Roby to do my chores," Harry says. "This is the wire that makes him do that. It must have shorted out."

"Less talking and more working,"
Ms. Lane says. "We can't hold him
forever."

Harry pulls out the wire. Super
Roby stops moving.

Harry and Macy high five. Ms. Lane shakes her head.

"See Superhero Harry? You did save the day!" Macy says.

"Harry Cruz, please come to the principal's office," says a voice from the loudspeaker. "Calling Harry Cruz."

It's Principal Banner.

"Go ahead, Harry," Ms. Lane says.

Harry drags his feet all the way to Principal Banner's office. This is not how the day was supposed to go.

Harry's parents are already with Prinicpal Banner. That is not a good sign.

"Harry, you caused quite a bit of trouble with your robot today," Principal Banner says.

"Harry, what happened?" his dad asks.

"I don't like chores. I made Super Roby so he would do my chores for me," Harry says.

"Harry, nobody likes doing chores," his mom says. "But it's something we all have to do. Even parents do chores."

"Superheroes don't have to do chores!" Harry says.

"Of course they do, Harry," Principal Banner says.

"They do?" Harry asks.

"Think about it," she says. "Do superheroes use their superpowers to vacuum, fold laundry, or do other things they can easily do themselves?"

"No, I guess not," Harry says.

"They use their powers for more important things," Principal Banner says. "Like helping people in need."

"I'm really sorry for all the trouble Super Roby and I caused today," Harry says. "And now I know a better way to use Super Roby."

"What is that?" his mom asks.

"We are going to help grandma clean her house," Harry says.

"That's a great idea, Harry!" his dad says.

"Let's get going!" Harry says.

"Superhero Harry, over and out!"

The Wild Field Trip

CHAPTER 1

THE LATEST INVENTION

Harry's school bus will be here any minute. He should be getting ready for the zoo field trip. Instead he's finishing up his latest superhero invention.

Harry LOVES superheroes. He wishes he had superpowers. But he's just a normal kid.

Harry builds inventions to make him more like a superhero. Harry's inventions don't always work. But he never stops trying.

Once he invented supersonic headphones. He used earmuffs, two empty soup cans, and a long string. The string was so long, Harry got tangled up in it and fell down.

Another time Harry made super stilt legs to help him reach things. He used what he thought were empty coffee cans and old bungee cords.

But the coffee cans were not empty. Harry left a trail of coffee from the kitchen to his room. His dad was not happy.

Harry's latest invention was perfect for the class field trip to the zoo. He had been working on the it for weeks!

Harry's favorite animals are monkeys. And monkeys swing from branch to branch. So Harry built an invention that will help him be a super swinger just like a monkey! It was his best idea yet!

Harry made wristbands with a button in the center of each. When he presses the button, wires shoot out. Each wristband has one wire.

The wires have coat hanger hooks
attached to their ends. The hooks
should grab onto tree branches.

Once the hooks attach, Harry will be able to swing like a monkey. At least that's how Harry hopes they will work.

"Harry!" his mom calls. "The bus is here!"

"Coming!" Harry says.

CHAPTER 2

SUPER SWINGER WRISTBANDS

"Over here, Harry!" says Macy.

Macy is Harry's next-door neighbor, superhero sidekick, classmate, and best friend. She always saves him a seat on the bus. Harry sits down next to her.

"What are those?" Macy asks, looking at the wristbands.

"My latest invention," Harry says proudly. "I call them the super swinger wristbands."

"How do they work?" Macy asks.

Harry explains his latest invention to Macy.

"So you've tested them out already?" she asks.

"Not yet," Harry says. "But I know they'll work."

"I don't know, Harry," Macy says.

But Harry says, "Trust me."

When they arrive at the zoo, Harry's class visits the giraffes first.

Jason stands on his tiptoes and stretches his neck to try and look like a giraffe.

Next they visit the penguins.

"Look at those cute little guys!"

Macy says. "They look like they're

wearing tuxedos!"

As the penguins waddle around,
Ethan and Jackson pin their arms to
their sides and waddle like penguins.

Then they go to the bird habitat.
Harry looks at the birds flying up
above.

"Next time I'll invent super flying wristbands. Then I can fly with the birds," Harry says.

"What are those?" Violet asks, pointing at Harry's wristbands.

"Are we talking about Harry's super swinging wristbands?" asks Macy.

"What are super swinging wristbands?" Melanie asks.

"Harry's latest invention," Macy says.

"How do they work, Harry?" Jackson asks.

"You'll see when we get to the monkeys, right Harry?" Macy says.

"That's right," Harry says. "Be prepared. Something really amazing is going to happen!"

CHAPTER 3

MR. BUNNY BUNNY

After lunch, the moment Harry has been waiting for finally arrives.

"All right, students," Ms. Lane says. "The next stop is the primate habitat. Everyone stay together."

Harry is so excited. He looks around and sees a lot of good trees for swinging. He decides it's time to test out his latest invention.

But Harry gets distracted when he hears a little girl crying.

She keeps saying, "Mr. Bunny Bunny! Mr. Bunny Bunny!"

She's pointing to her stuffed bunny. It's on the other side of the fence. Her dad is busy talking to another adult. He doesn't even notice!

"She must have thrown it over,"
Harry says quietly. "This seems like
a job for Superhero Harry. After all,
superheroes should save the day!"

The stuffed bunny isn't too far from the fence. Harry tries to grab it. But his arm is too big to fit under the fence.

Next he finds a long tree branch. He tries to sweep the stuffed bunny toward the fence. But that doesn't work either.

"Wait a minute," Harry says. "My super swinging wristbands will be perfect for this!"

Harry pushes the button on his right wristband. The wire shoots out. One of the coat hanger hooks grabs Mr. Bunny Bunny.

Harry presses the button again to make the wire come back. It does! Mr. Bunny Bunny flies right over the fence!

Once Mr. Bunny Bunny is safely in his arms, he gives it to the sweet little girl.

She gives Mr. Bunny Bunny a big hug. Then she gives Harry a big hug.

Harry can't believe he did it! His invention actually works!

CHAPTER 4

MONKEY MADNESS

"Harry, there you are!" Macy says. "Everyone else already moved ahead."

"You missed it, Macy!" Harry says. "I just saved a little girl's stuffed bunny. I used my cool wristbands and everything. I was a real superhero!"

"Your invention really works?"
Macy says. "You have to show me!"

"Get ready, monkeys," Harry
says. "Here I come!"

Harry aims one wristband at the
closest tree. He pushes the button.
Nothing happens. He pushes
the button again. Still, nothing
happens.

"You said it worked," Macy says.

"It does!" Harry says. "Let me try
it one more time. It might just be
stuck."

He pushes the button again.

This time a wire shoots out. But it doesn't hook onto the tree. Instead it hooks around a little monkey's leg!

Without thinking, Harry pushes the button again. The scared little monkey comes flying over the fence.

It safely lands in a small bush.

At the same time, the wire on

Harry's wristband breaks.

"This is bad," Harry says.

"Real bad."

"What are we going to do?"
Macy asks.

"We have to fix this," Harry
says. "And we have to do it fast."

"How?" Macy asks.

"Just follow me," Harry says.

CHAPTER 5

THE BANANA

Harry runs over to the little monkey. Macy is close behind him. The monkey is all tangled up in the wire and the bush.

Harry quickly untangles the monkey. Then he gives him a banana. The little monkey doesn't look scared anymore.

"Do you always carry around a banana?" Macy asks.

"I do when I'm going to the zoo," Harry says. "You never know when you might need it."

"Now what do we do?" Macy asks.

"We swing," Harry says.

"I have no idea what you are talking about," Macy says.

"Just watch," Harry says.

He takes off the broken wristband. He climbs on a bench and carefully holds the monkey.

Harry pushes the button on his left wristband. The wire shoots out. It misses the tree. Harry tries again. It misses again.

"I don't think this is going to work," Macy says.

"It will work! Third time is a charm!" Harry says.

This time the wire hits the tree. It sticks to the branch! Harry and the monkey fly over the fence, swinging from the tree.

"You did it!" Macy yells.

The monkey climbs onto the branch. Harry climbs onto the branch too. Now Harry just needs to get out.

Harry takes the hook from the super swinger out of the tree. He pulls the wire back into his wristband. Harry aims it at a tree on the other side of the fence.

He takes a deep breath and pushes the button. It grips on the first time!

"Hurry, Harry!" Macy yells.

Harry jumps and swings to safety. As he swings, Harry gets all tangled up in the wire. His landing is a mess, but he did it.

His invention really works!

"That was so cool," Macy says. "And now we have to hurry. The bus is here!"

"Roger that," Harry says.

Macy helps Harry untangle the wire. Macy is extra good at it since she is always untangling her necklaces.

"Come on, Harry! We are going to miss the bus!" Macy yells.

Harry and Macy run through the zoo. They pass the giraffes. They pass the lions. They pass the penguins.

"I wish you had invented something to make us fly," Macy says. "That would be really handy right now!"

"I'm working on it," Harry says, huffing and puffing. "One invention at a time."

They get to the bus, quietly climb on, and sit down. Ms. Lane looks suspicious but doesn't say anything.

"Now that we have everyone we can head back," Ms. Lane tells the bus driver.

"This was one wild field trip," Macy says.

"It sure was! I can't wait to get started on my next superhero invention," Harry says.

"What are you going to make next?" Macy asks.

"I'm not sure, but I know it's going to be cool. Superhero Harry, over and out!" he says.

ABOUT THE AUTHOR

Rachel Ruiz is the author of several children's books. She was inspired to write her first picture book, When Penny met POTUS, after working for Barack Obama on his re-election campaign in 2012.

When Rachel isn't writing books, she writes and produces TV shows and documentaries. She lives in her hometown of Chicago with her husband and their daughter.

ABOUT THE ARTIST

Steve May is a professional illustrator and animation director. He says he spent his childhood drawing lots of things and discovering interesting ways of injuring himself.

Steve's work has become a regular feature in the world of children's books. He still draws lots but injures himself less regularly now. He lives in glamorous north London, and his mom says he's a genius.